Huntingdon, ~

Dad's Dodgy Lodger

Philip Wooderson and Dee Shulman

A & C Black · London

JUMBO JETS

First published 1997 by A&C Black (Publishers) Ltd
35 Bedford Row, London WC1R 4JH

ISBN 0-7136-4790-6

A CIP catalogue record for this book
is available from the British Library.

Photoset by Rowland Phototypesetting Ltd
Bury St Edmunds, Suffolk
Printed in Great Britain by
William Clowes Ltd, Beccles and London

I've got a surprise.

Dad grinned, as if I was bound to be pleased.

That's funny—so have I, Dad.

'What's your surprise?' Dad asked.

I told him our teacher, Mr Leonnard, wanted us all to turn up in home-made Easter bonnets on the last day of term, in two weeks. He wanted them

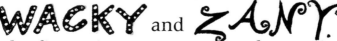 **WACKY** and **ZANY**.

The first prize was a weekend away in the headmistress's holiday cottage.

3

Dad did his best to keep grinning.

Why should I mind? I knew we needed
the money. Besides, Dad had worked
for days repainting the back bedroom,
putting up new curtains, even buying a
Teasmade. Now somebody must have
replied to his advert in the local paper.
I was intrigued.

'One small problem,' said Dad.
'This lodger wants a front room.'

Dad went a bit red round the ears.
'You told me you liked the back room.'

My front room was grubby and pokey.
'But why shouldn't he like it too,
Dad?'

Dad tilted his head to one side.

CHAPTER TWO

Our French Lodger-ess

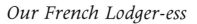

How glamorous! How exciting!!
Though why would she want to come
here? Dad hadn't a clue, he just worried
about what she'd want for breakfast.

Dad spent
the next
hour shifting
stuff from my
room, but it
was still
shabby and
cramped.

As for my new
bedroom, it
was more than
twice the size,
with a view
down our
garden to the
tall trees at the
bottom, hiding
the railway line
and the road on
the other side.

What sort of weirdo French girl would
rather look out on our High Street, with
all those boring shops like:

What if she changed her mind?

Downstairs, I found Dad busy sketching. In fact, he's a brilliant artist, and when he's got a job, it's working backstage in theatres, painting the scenery. So I didn't have any doubts he could dream up the right sort of bonnet for our Easter Parade.

Dad sketched it, and added some chicks.

But before I could tell him I liked it,
the doorbell chimed. Our French girl?

We both rushed to open the door.

Some French *girl*! She looked as old as Dad.

Before all her stuff was indoors, she sailed on into our kitchen, picked up Dad's sketch book and squealed,

I thought I'd better explain about our Easter Parade. But Mini flipped back a page to Dad's first wacky sketch – 'Your dad – he did this too? I love it!'

But people would laugh at me.

Let them. Take risks! That's why I'm here.

We waited to hear why that was, but Mini just beamed at us both, as if it was perfectly clear. And rather than make any comment, Dad started burbling on about how well she spoke English, and how he was lousy at French, and what about . . .

. . . Some strong coffee, or maybe an English cheese sandwich?

She ended up having both . . .

. . . followed by fruit cake and biscuits.

Then she got Dad and I to lug her luggage upstairs. It wouldn't all fit in 'her' room. Some had to be stacked on the landing.

The room is so small . . .

Mini said.

You wanted the front room!

Dad said.

Why did you want it?

I put in.

Dad glowered at me. 'That's enough, Sophie.'

Mini sat on 'her' bed and bounced up and down.

No! No!

From your window I hope to see all the life in the street.

Downstairs I looked hard at Dad, waiting to hear what he thought about our French lodgeress. But Dad wouldn't meet my eyes.

CHAPTER THREE

Settling in

Next morning Dad had to go shopping, to stock up for Mini's first breakfast. He was back by eight-thirty, but Mini stayed locked in the bathroom, running off all the hot water and filling the house with steam. By half-past nine Dad was wondering if he should take her breakfast upstairs.

Mini thought she could manage a spot.

She managed:

I couldn't resist it. 'So where do you work?' I demanded.

I work in the Arts —

— Once as a dancer —in big shows—

—but I got too old so I moved on into theatres—

You mean you're an actress?

I gasped.

Dad was glaring at me.

'No, no, it is a good question.' She
munched up the last bit of toast.
'I have a confession to make.'

What was she going to tell us?

'Well, neither do I,'
Dad admitted.

It took us a moment to get this.

She managed a brave sort of smile.

Before Dad could think what to say next, she got to her feet.

'You are **so kind**, because you understand, because we are both artists.'

She reached for his sketch of a hat with big floppy ears. 'I love this, but you must be bolder. A whole furry head of a rabbit for Sophie to wear like a mask!'

'No thanks,' I said quickly.

'I will help make it,' said Mini. 'And help round the house, pay my way!'

'Uh?...' 'Hummmm.'

CHAPTER FOUR

Doubts about Dad

I didn't believe in her 'prospects'.
Why should they have to be secret? But
Dad said we ought to be patient and
stand by friends in trouble . . .

She isn't our **friend**.

I mean, we don't even **know** her.

The poor girl's only just come here. She doesn't know anyone else.

She's not a girl! What are you drawing?

I can't wear **that**!

'Why not?'

'It's Mini's idea. It even looks like her.'

This whole thing was getting me down.

Mini hoovered up
Dad's big breakfasts,

snacked from
the fridge
at night,

kept using our washing machine, and
ran off tanks of hot water taking two
baths every day. What's more, she
NEVER went out.

It's for
Mini.

I knocked on her door and shouted, but she had the radio on, blasting out opera music. What's more, the door was bolted. So I peered through the keyhole. I saw a strange woman in black!

I called over the banister,

Dad, she's got someone else in there!

Dad clomped up the stairs, looking puzzled.

What's wrong with that? She can have friends.

You said she hadn't got any friends. Look!

Dad wouldn't. He knocked on the door, and kept on knocking away until Mini opened it. She was wearing her baggy mauve dress. I tried looking into the room, but she slammed the door behind her.

She stayed on the phone for a long time, whispering into the mouthpiece so I couldn't hear what she said.

But when she put the phone down she had a sly grin on her face.

Mini asked with her
eyes wide.

"What friend?"

"You two are my only friends here."

Dad shook his head at me.
'You've been imagining things.'

Mini got through three
helpings of curry, and polished
off two bowls of ice cream.

"May I ask you one small thing?"

"Anything, Mini."

She opened her eyes extra wide.

I think I'll be having more phone calls. And as this is all so important, I'd rather take them in private.

Dad's jaw flapped.

Of course—

I should have thought.

You have a phone point upstairs?

It made me really cross to see Dad unplugging our phone. Mini soon had it shut in her room. What's more, when I went to bed, I heard her talking away when I knew the phone hadn't rung. So unless her friend was still in there, she was making long phone calls at our expense.

Thanks a lot!

CHAPTER FIVE

Things get even odder

I managed to put it to Dad, while Mini was in the bath.

She might be phoning France!

You wait till you see the phone bill.

Ooh, she'll pay us back.

Dad was breezy. (Too breezy by half. He was worried.)

She can't even pay the rent, Dad!

She said she would next week.

Depending on her prospects.

She's not gone to look for a job, Dad! She never goes out of the house!

That's none of our business. We'll leave it a few more days.

So that was that. I was late, but as I set off for school, I looked up at my old bedroom window and there she was, peering out.

What was she so intrigued by? All I could see were old ladies pushing shopping trollies.

As soon as I got to school I talked to my best friend Karen. She didn't have any doubts.

That sounded more likely to me.
Though she was too old for a
BOYfriend. Much more likely a mad
old man. This would explain the phone
calls – and her not leaving the house.

Dad needed to hear about this. But
when I got home from school, he
wasn't there. Mini was, on the phone

again, upstairs. And
this time she'd left
her door open, so I
heard what she said.

I think we rendez-vous, Thursday, four-thirty, at Veggies Cafe? And if all is well, I can go, Kurt, I hope, on Friday morning.

I found Dad in his shed. But what I saw there left me speechless.

Wait till they're covered in fur. You'll love 'em.

He told me he had talked to Mini while
I'd been out at school, and she'd had
the clever idea of selling them to a
toy shop . . .

'To "help"?' I could hardly believe this.

I glared at him, opened my mouth, then shut it again, feeling hopeless. I'd do better talking to Karen. I called round to her house.

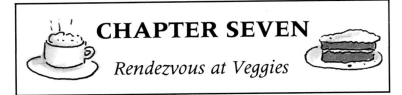

CHAPTER SEVEN

Rendezvous at Veggies

On Thursday we got to the cafe a little bit after four-thirty, peered through the steamy window, and saw Mini, sitting alone.

No sign of mysterious Kurt, though.

Hold on —

She tugged my wrist as a car like a silver fish came nosing over the kerb.

So Karen shot in by herself. I found a
doorway and waited, wondering what I
was missing.

When Karen came out she looked jaunty.

I was out of my depth. But something
had to be done. And for the very first
time, Mini was out of the house.

CHAPTER EIGHT

Looking and learning

Both of us crept upstairs and tried her door. It was locked. But Dad was not at home either, so I slipped into his bedroom and picked up his bunch of spare keys. The third key I tried slotted in. The lock clicked, the door creaked open. We stepped into Mini's room.

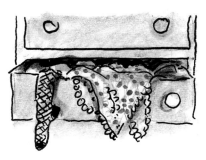

We looked through the chest of drawers, turning out Mini-style clothes. Next we moved on to the holdalls.

In these there were dancing costumes, and albums of photos of Mini wearing her dancing gear.

So some of her stories were true.

'Hey, Sophie?' From under the bed, Karen had brought out a bundle of black clothes, along with a black baseball cap. 'Were these what her friend was wearing?'

I thought back to what I had seen, through the keyhole. It must have been Mini I'd caught sight of, squashed into those black clothes. Then she had changed out of them before she had opened the door.

I looked at the page more carefully.
This had to be her escape route. 'Just
wait till Dad sees this!'

Karen gasped.

Sssh.

Listen, Sophie.
Someone's coming
upstairs!

We swopped
horrified glances.

WHAT ON EARTH ARE
YOU TWO UP TO?

I let out my breath. It was Dad.

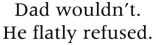

Come and see what we've found here.

Dad wouldn't.
He flatly refused.

Mini's our lodger, Sophie. You've no right —

And she's no right either.

She's only been waiting for kurt, and now she's ready to flit off without

I would have said 'paying', but that's when I noticed Mini, hovering in the doorway. She must have been following Dad.

Interesting question, Sophie. Serge needs someone unknown, not too young, with fuzzy hair, to play a has-been French dancer, with a crazy boyfriend planning to rob a bank.
She lives in a grotty bedsit. That's why I stay here... to get a feel for the part. I pretend to myself I'm hiding – watching the street, writing notes.
GROTTY BEDSIT?!
Planning getaway routes...
... and wearing black clothes!

Mini kept nodding away. 'Now Kurt's arranged my audition. For 9.45am on Friday. And Kurt has good things for your dad too.'

'Dad can't act!'

'He wouldn't be acting Sophie!'

'He'd only be painting sets!'

'And Kurt has a friend with a toyshop who wants your dad's rabbit masks. So cheer up. Our luck is changing!'

I hoped so. I hoped it rained money. But surely . . ?

One thing WAS certain. Mini must have an audition, or else she wouldn't be offering to take Dad along to meet Kurt. So she wouldn't escape without paying us, at least not on Friday morning.

'But Friday's tomorrow – it's the Easter Parade.'

 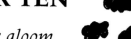
I stayed in my room feeling gloomy,
listening to Dad and Mini laughing
away in the kitchen. They were having
a wonderful time, and when I went
down I found out why. They'd been
hard at work on Dad's masks.

'Amazing, Dad,' I admitted, not feeling
terribly pleased as he slipped one over
my head.

43

The trouble is I can't see, and... I don't think it's really Eastery.

But you're an Easter bunny!

Except—

I tugged the thing off.

—Its ears look more like worms!

That moment the phone bleeped and Mini rushed out of the kitchen, calling over her shoulder,

It will be Kurt. I'll go upstairs.

Dad pointed at a container.

Your mask's not finished yet, Sophie. The ears will be filled up with this stuff.

He peeled the mask inside out and slapped on a thick coat of latex, using a tablespoon to fill up the ears. 'When it's dried off, you'll find it's all soft and bendy.'

When will that be?

Not for hours. Now how about doing the others?

I'm hungry.

All right, they can wait till the morning. Let's cook some ham and eggs.

In the morning, Mini told Dad what Kurt had told her last night . . . 'Kurt's friend is coming this morning to pick up the masks for the shop.'

But we won't be here.

It's no problem. I said we'd leave the key under the dustbin outside, and leave the masks on the hall table.

Bu-But- the masks haven't been filled with latex, and we've got to go straight away.

I'll do it— I've got time, Dad, before I go to school.

Dad frowned.

You'd have to be careful — the masks will take hours to dry.

I'll write them a warning. Don't worry.

Dad didn't have any choice. Mini hurried him out of the house. And I got down to work, filling all the ears with lashings of creamy latex. Gobbets got stuck to my fingers, and wouldn't come off.

Then the front door bell chimed.

Karen was wearing her bonnet.

It made me ill with envy.

But while I was rattling on about how lucky she was, she pushed me out through the front door.

Crowds of parents had turned up, all hoping their child would win, because they'd all spent several evenings hard at work on their bonnets.

The judges sat down in the front row, while we all queued backstage, waiting to go on. I kept my silly bunny head stuffed in its carrier bag, too embarrassed to put it on until the very last moment. But Mr Leonnard loved it.

Wonderful, Sophie. So **wacky** and **zany!**

Except it's not really a bonnet.

I still couldn't see through the eyeholes.
But the music blared out. Off we went,
thirty-eight Easter bonnets, one at a time
down the catwalk. The audience tittered
and . . . CLAPPED AT ME?!

We had to wait for the judges to settle
on six for the next round, then
Mr Leonnard called out the names.

As he called my name, a burglar alarm went off somewhere outside.

WOODLE WOODLE
WOODLE
WOODLE

I felt too hot.
I felt dizzy.
I wanted to
get my mask
off and breathe
some fresh air.

But Mr Leonnard was
clapping his hands.

On parade again,
if you don't mind.

WOODLE WOODLE

The audience cheered louder than the burglar alarm. But when Mr Leonnard called for silence, to help the judges to think straight, we could hear sirens as well, getting closer and closer. What was happening out there?

WOODLE WOODLE

NEE-NAW NEE-NAW

In reverse order. The third prize goes to Ben. Well done!

HOORAY

Second prize goes to Mandy!

HOORAY! HOORAY!

And the winner...

BOO!

HOORAY!

BOO! HOORAY!

And the winner...

Wild chatter broke out in the hall.
The headmistress was calling,

But people were standing up now,
crowding against the window.

I couldn't see much through the
eyeholes, but Karen was tugging my
sleeve. Then somebody opened the fire
doors and she pulled me outside with
the others.

My bonnet just wouldn't come off. While everyone else was scooping up money I was trying to get off my 'bonnet', tugging at the ears and pulling hard on the snout. But the wretched thing had shrunk. I found myself by the school gate. The High Street was full of policemen.

EXCUSE me, what's happening?

The policeman gargled,

Lads closed in from all directions, crushing me into a corner, and suddenly I was in handcuffs.

What me? I was struggling for breath, mouth full of furry latex. I screamed, nearly deafening myself, but none of them seemed to hear. They bundled me into a van and off we went at top speed.

And when we got to the station, they guided me down a passage with doors on either side with thick iron bars in their windows. Cells! 'No — please!' I cried. 'There's been an awful mistake!'

'That's what your friends said.'

'What friends?' I asked.

I got it. Those masks, remember? I'd filled them up with latex but I'd forgotten to leave any warning about it still being sticky. Kurt's friends at the toyshop must have tried them on, then panicked and called the police. Did they reckon I'd done it on purpose?

I did my best to explain, but through my mask I could see all the policemen smirking, as if I was having them on.

This wasn't what I'd expected, being sat down to watch telly. But as soon as the video started it suddenly all made sense.

CHAPTER THIRTEEN

To cut a long story short

That evening, we sat in the kitchen, eating Chinese food from the take-away in the High Street.

The police had been talking to Mini for most of the afternoon, but now she was back.

It was crazy! They thought I'd been helping those **thieves**! They thought Kurt was my **boyfriend**!

Mini looked strangely amazed.

It's been a peculiar day!

They giggled. I stared at them both,
amazed by how weird grown-ups
can be.

I'd heard the whole sorry tale. Dad and
Mini had reached the studio only to
learn that Serge Goldflank was making
a film in Las Vegas and wasn't in need
of an actress.

No-one had
heard of 'Kurt'.

I'm sorry –
this 'kurt'
doesn't even
work in the
kitchen!

GOLDFLANK STUDIOS

Of course, Mini wasn't a crook, just someone Kurt had been conning.

He'd got her to stay in our house to make her watch the High Street, 'to get a feel for her part'.

By noting all comings and goings, she had helped him fix on the best time to mount his raid on the BEDROCK.

FRIDAY
9.30 Girl with black hair arrives.
9.32 Man with glasses arrives.
10.00 Security van arrives 2 men unload metal boxes.
10.15 Security van leaves.
1 pm. Girl with black hair goes to lunch.
2 pm. Girl with black hair returns
3pm Man with glasses goes out.

I told him when the money arrived!

With all of us out of the house and the door key under the dustbin his gang had the perfect escape route, over the railway line.

I had to smile. But then I remembered Mini wanting that part in the film, and Dad so desperately needing to get a new job painting scenery. We'd all been conned by that rogue. And now we were back to square one – without any money or even 'prospects'. In fact it was sad. It was tragic. So why were Dad and Mini acting as if it was Christmas???

Dad raised a glass.

Dad eased himself back in his chair, as if to tell a long story. But instead he just let out his breath and said in a satisfied way,

Kurt did us some good as it happens. The film people thought it was funny.

And as it turns out they do need a person to help with stage sets. So they said they'd give me a try.

What's more, they're short of a waitress in their canteen. So we're both fixed!

Mini laughed.

Do you know, they were holding hands now. I looked at them, slightly puzzled. But they were looking so happy, I told them *my* good news. 'We won the Easter Bonnet Parade,' I said. 'We can all have a weekend away . . .'